Chameleons

The Mean Team from Mars

Written and illustrated by
Scoular Anderson

A & C Black • London

For Mark and Blair

First published 2003 by
A & C Black Publishers Ltd
37 Soho Square, London, W1D 3QZ

www.acblack.com

ISBN 0-7136-6437-1

A CIP catalogue for this book is available from the British Library.

A&C Black uses paper produced with elemental chlorine-free
pulp, harvested from managed sustained forests.

Printed and bound in Singapore by Tien Wah Press (Pte) Ltd

Chapter 1

It was Tuesday. The Arden Under-eights were training for their big match against the team from Skellyhall.

Rory went in to tackle and ...

Mr Mint blew his whistle.

Rory spent the rest of the match standing
on the touchline.

The next Tuesday, Rory got into trouble again ...

... and again the Tuesday after that.

The following week, Rory kicked one of the other players.

Mr Mint blew his whistle so hard it made
Rory's ears rattle.

PHEEEeeeEP!

Mr Mint reached
into his pocket ...

... and brought
out a real
red card.

Chapter 2

At last the day of the big match came.
Rory laid out his kit on the bed.

His mum put her head round the door.

The market was busy. Rory's mum went off to buy vegetables.

Rory had saved up nine pounds and fifty pence and he looked around for something to buy.

Rory pulled out his wallet.

Rory was feeling
really pleased
with himself …

… until he
met his mum.

Oh Rory, not more of
that stuff! You're not
wasting your money
on that! We'll take
it back.

Rory took her to the place where he had bought the duvet cover. But the stall wasn't there.

That's funny. It's vanished.

Oh, never mind. Let's go home.

Back home, Rory rushed to his room with his new duvet cover. He had a collection of Arden United things. He had Arden United curtains ...

Arden United pens ...

... and pencil case.

He had an Arden United rug …

… and towel.

He even had
Arden United
underpants.

Now he had an Arden
United duvet cover.
He pulled the cover
out of the packet and
spread it on the bed.

It was amazing. There was the Arden
United pitch laid out in front of him.

He was very excited. He took a deep
breath and jumped on to the pitch.

Chapter 3

OUCH!

Rory didn't land on a soft duvet on top
of a soft bed. His new duvet cover
seemed to be as hard as …

A football
pitch?

Rory sat up. There was real grass under his hands and a real grandstand in front of him.

He was right in the middle of Arden United Football Ground.

There was something strange about the place. He looked up and saw what it was. The whole football pitch was covered by a glass roof.

That wasn't there last week!

... and had four arms ...

... and four legs.

Skrekie and Rory kicked the ball to one another as they ran down the pitch.

Just then, someone else came on to the pitch.

Mr Migg came across to Rory.

Mr Migg gave Rory a funny look.

Chapter 4

The glass roof above the stadium opened. A spaceship came through slowly. It came down and landed on the pitch.

The doors of the bus opened. The Mars North School team got out and walked to the changing room. Rory's eyes almost fell out of his head. If these kids were the Under-eights, he was in for a hard match.

Skrekie saw Rory stare at the visiting team.

The game began. Rory and Skrekie did well. They were small and nimble. They ran rings round the Drabonians …

WHOOSH!

… and the Plutonians …

… and even the Swurling in goal.

Then Rory had a little trouble from the Belovian.

Rory fell to the ground. **Oww! My knee!**

The referee blew his whistle. A big red card began to flash above the stadium.

Something very strange happened next.
A long tube came down from the top of
the stadium.

A voice boomed out ...

MARS NORTH SCHOOL,
NUMBER 2 – TO THE
SIN-BIN!

Then the Belovian was
sucked up, like a bit of
fluff, into a hoover.

Just after Rory scored his third goal,
the final whistle went.

The final score came up on the
scoreboard …

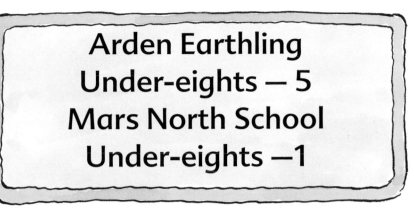

**Arden Earthling
Under-eights — 5
Mars North School
Under-eights —1**

The teams began
to walk off the
pitch. Rory and
Skrekie gave a
big leap of joy.

35

Chapter 5

Rory landed on something hard for the second time that day. It was his bedroom floor.

Skrekie landed on top of him.

Just then, Rory saw
the time on the clock
beside his bed.

Rory pointed to his Arden United calendar.

Rory clasped his knee. The tackle from
the big Belovian had made it really sore.

Rory looked Skrekie up and down.

Skrekie needed a disguise. Rory thought about it …

Some of his mum's face powder made
Skrekie less green.

Skrekie hid a pair of
arms under his shirt.

Jogging pants
hid his legs well.

Skrekie's feet
were small.
Rory's feet
were big.

Skrekie squeezed his
four feet into Rory's boots.

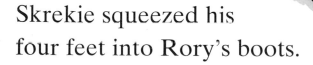

At last, Skrekie was ready.

The two boys sneaked out of the back door.

At the football ground, Rory saw Skrekie staring at the pitch.

Skrekie stared at the visiting team.

Rory kept out of sight. Skrekie ran on to the pitch at the last moment. Mr Mint didn't notice anything strange.

He started the game.

Chapter 6

Skrekie ran rings round the team from Skellyhall. He scored four goals.

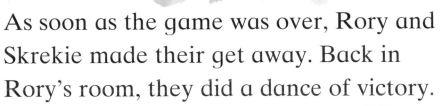

As soon as the game was over, Rory and Skrekie made their get away. Back in Rory's room, they did a dance of victory.

We won!

We won!

Skrekie jumped and fell on the bed …

… and vanished.

Rory's mum put her head round the door.

Mr Mint was all smiles.

Mr Mint went away and Rory ran upstairs. He just had to tell Skrekie what had happened. He could jump on to his duvet and into the future for just a minute …

… but the duvet cover wasn't there.

Just then, he heard his mum call him. He ran downstairs.

His mum had just emptied the washing machine.

Rory shrugged. He wouldn't be doing any more time-travel, that was for sure.